I a~
but you're
the Coolest

I am Cool, but You're the Coolest

Copyright © 2021 Demesiner and Massah Patrick

Paperback ISBN: 978-1-7375096-6-0
Hardcover ISBN: 978-1-7375096-7-7

10 9 8 7 6 5 4 3 2 1
Printed in the United States

Priceless Publishing®
Coral Springs, Fl
www.pricelesspublishing.co

DEDICATION

To our dearest children,

You are a **PATRICK**
Honorably and with pride
Purposely placed to teach and be taught
We will all protect and respect our family's name
If one member suffers, we all suffer together;
if one member is honored, we all rejoice together
Patrick's are hard-working and loyal
Our only fear is God himself.

**AS LONG AS YOU ARE "ALWAYS WILLING"
YOU WILL ALWAYS SUCCEED.**

I AM NOT READY FOR THE FIRST DAY OF SCHOOL.
I AM NOT READY BECAUSE I AM NOT THAT COOL.

WHAT DO YOU MEAN YOU'RE NOT READY FOR SCHOOL?
WHAT DO YOU MEAN YOU ARE NOT THAT COOL?

I WILL HAVE TO RIDE THE BUS TO SCHOOL.
THE KIDS ON THE BUS ARE OH, SO COOL.

THEN I WILL HAVE TO GO TO CLASS,
SO MUCH TO DO — MATH, SCIENCE,
EVEN ARTS AND CRAFT!

AND WHO WILL I SIT WITH WHEN IT'S TIME FOR LUNCH?
THE COOL KIDS WILL BE GROUPED UP,
SITTING IN A BUNCH.

THE COOL KIDS GIGGLE, LAUGH AND PLAY ALL DAY,
RUNNING, SKIPPING AND JUMPING,
BUT THEY NEVER SAY 'HEY!'.

DADDY, DADDY, CAN YOU COME TO MY SCHOOL?
PLEASE DADDY, YOU ARE OH, SO COOL!

YES, I WILL COME WITH YOU FOR THE
FIRST DAY OF SCHOOL. BUT I PROMISE
YOU MY DEAR CHILD, YOU TOO ARE COOL.

.

DON'T WORRY YOUR LITTLE HEAD ABOUT YOUR FIRST DAY OF SCHOOL. EVERYTHING'S ALL SET — NEVER FORGET YOU TOO ARE COOL.

WITH A RIDE ON THE BUS, THE SCHOOL YEAR BEGINS.
YOU WILL MAKE FRIENDS AND CHAT
ABOUT MANY THINGS.

SUCH A GOOD TIME YOU WILL MAKE IN CLASS.

BOLD QUESTIONS YOU WILL ANSWER AND ASK.

SIT WITH YOUR CLASS WHEN IT'S TIME FOR LUNCH.
ENJOY YOUR FOOD WITH A GREAT BIG CRUNCH.

SHOW ME YOUR MUSCLES, YOU'RE SO BIG AND STRONG!

YOU TOO CAN LAUGH AND PLAY,

ALL DAY LONG!

TRUST ME I KNOW YOU WILL DO WELL AT SCHOOL.
I KNOW YOU WILL BECAUSE YOU HAVE THE RIGHT TOOLS

SO PLEASE, MY DEAR CHILD, JUST GET SOME REST.
TOMORROW AT SCHOOL PROMISE ME YOU'LL
GIVE IT YOUR BEST. AND REMEMBER

I AM COOL, BUT YOU ARE THE COOLEST.

ABOUT THE AUTHORS

DEMESINER AND MASSAH PATRICK are a married couple who met in Kuwait. They have two children and made it their life's mission to ensure they were their children's primary source of education. Both members of this couple are military veterans and share the desire to help and mentor people, especially young people and children. The title of their first book **"I AM COOL BUT YOU ARE THE COOLEST"** was inspired by an affirmation between the parents and their children.

Lightning Source UK Ltd.
Milton Keynes UK
UKHW050922060921
390005UK00002B/15